THE SHADOW COVE INCIDENT
and Other Suspenseful Stories

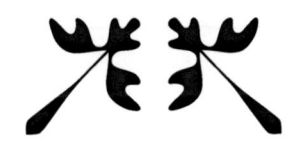

Jeanne Wray

The Shadow Cove Incident and Other Suspenseful Stories

Copyright © 2012 by Jeanne Wray

All rights reserved. No part of this book may be reproduced or transmitted in any form or by any means without written permission of the author.

ISBN 978162050148

ACKNOWLEDGEMENTS

Cover painting by Jeanne Wray

I would like to dedicate this book to my daughter, Jill Bondy who encouraged me to write after I no longer could paint. If it wasn't for her I don't think I would have gone on with my writing. Thank you to The Golden Pen Writers for being there and encouraging me. I never could have accomplished this without you.

Greg and Melissa
May God watch over you and your family
Jeanne Wray

Contents

The Shadow Cove Incident 1
Shadow Cove Incident 1
Joseph Bareille 23
Another Time 33
One Spring Afternoon 37
Legacy 47
Bessie 53
End Of A Journey 59
Carla Shannon 65
The Arrival 71
The Meeting 77
Future/ Destiny 83
Stories to Muse Over 89

PROLOGUE

He was tied hand and foot, unconscious lying in his boat. Blood was pooling under him. He was still alive. Some hours later beginning to surface from the deep abyss he had been in he became aware of a gentle rocking and the sound of water splashing. Where was he? Everything was blurred. How had he ended up here? Looking up he began to recognize some of his equipment hanging on the walls. Then he knew. He was in his boathouse in the cove at the bottom of the property where his home stood.

The last he remembered, he was with his brother when they went to the bank to get money, a lot of it. *It was the only way to get rid of him.* His brother had always been trouble. *He should still have been in the penitentiary. Released sooner than expected. Must have overpowered me and brought me here after he got the cash. Good place to stash someone. No one ever comes down here except the caretaker and myself once a week.*

Can't move my arms – tied and pinned under me. My feet are tied too. He must have done this after I gave him the money. Now what? God, don't let him hurt my family. With the cash, maybe they'll leave now. The woman he brought with him gives me the creeps. Not all there. Have to get loose; get up to the house.

He heard the latch turn on the door. Someone was coming. Then a figure was silhouetted in the doorway. It was she.

Maybe come to let me out. That's tilting at windmills. He tried to speak and realized his mouth was taped. She approached the boat; he looked up into those crazy eyes and knew then that he should have kept his shut.

From out of that mouth came, "You wake. Too bad," then she hit him again and again with one of the oars.

It was some hours before he again surfaced into reality. He was weak, hurt all over and his mouth felt like cotton - he knew his nose was broken. The boat was rocking more than before. The sea must be rough. There was little light so it was probably near evening. He lay there drifting in and out of consciousness. Then something startled him and he was fully awake. The door was opening again...

SHADOW COVE INCIDENT

You could hear the eagerness in the girl's voice as she entered the room. "Jenna, please come with me. Ten days to just relax and have fun." The pretty blonde pouted and wiped away mock tears from her green eyes. The two were roommates at a university on the northern coast of California.

"Kara, you know I have last term's inventory to do and the books for next semester must be counted and distributed. I pay part of my tuition doing this. I would give anything to get away from here for a while. This comes first."

"I guess. But if you should change your mind, you have my cell number. You are more than welcome. Just think about the sea dashing up on the cliffs, fog coming in to cover the land in the evening, a nice cozy fire at night, hot cocoa and good friends." Kara tried tempting her redheaded friend whose hair matched her stubbornness. Jenna was average height and was trying to get on the swim team. She had brown eyes and quite a nice trim figure.

Jenna smiled and hugged her roommate. Saying a tearful goodbye she left to go to work. She arrived first. Tim Corby was to help also. Professor Derwich would be in charge. There was the inventory to take of books that could be used again this semester and distribution of new material to the classrooms in the Science Department. Just then, Tim came in.

The way he was breathing, he sounded like he had run all the way across campus. He was fair-haired and built on the lean side about five foot eleven and on the university's track team.

"This is a bummer, staying to do this all week instead of going off to the beach. Some of the guys are going down to Carmel. If we get through early I'm going to try to go and get a few days to party," Tim grumbled.

"Are you? Maybe I could hitch a ride part of the way. Kara invited me to stay at her parents' house this week. I had to say no because of the inventory. I don't have any transportation, so even if we do finish sooner I couldn't get away." Looking at him through her eyelashes Jenna asked. "Would you be so kind?"

Professor Derwich came in just then and Jenna did not get an answer to her question. They went right to work taking inventory; there were stacks of books to count. With the new supplies to distribute, this was going to take a lot of time. Then, on the second dreary day of work, the professor announced they were through. "What?" Tim and Jenna said in unison.

"We thought there was more material to go through," Tim said.

"There should be but it has not arrived and it won't be here for another two weeks. So it looks like you two will have some time off. Straighten up here and you can go. I don't want to see either of you until next week." He smiled.

Needless to say, things were put in order in record time. As Jenna was leaving, Tim came to her and said, "I can take you down to Kara's house, Shadow Cove is on my way, but be ready first thing in the morning, about seven. I don't want to leave tonight I have a few things to take care of."

Jenna was ecstatic. When she got Kara on her phone, they were both very excited at the turn of events. "I am going to go into town tomorrow morning and pick up Gracie but I will be home for rest of the day. See you then, Jenna."

◄◄►►

They started on time the next morning. Tim had a 1999 Ford Escort, in good shape mechanically. Not much could be said for its appearance. He was an expert mechanic, his family owned a garage and he had been raised around cars so he could fix almost anything.

The scenery along the coast was spectacular - there was something breathtaking around every turn. The high craggy cliffs soaring up into the cerulean blue sky and then disappearing down into the ever restless sea. It made you realize just how small one is in this world.

As they got closer to where Kara lived, they became aware of an abundance of gulls, pelicans and other seafowl. There was a small fishing settlement close by that attracted the bird population it was called Shadow Cove because of the large craggy cliffs among the trees on the east side of the town. They cast deep shadows down upon the village at different times during the day. Kara's house was about a mile beyond on a side road off the highway. The house sat alone upon a flat piece of land backing up to the caves and rock formations that disappeared into the sand and rolling surf.

They stopped in front of a large house whose architecture matched its locale. It was built to take advantage of the surroundings – driftwood and castaway shells were scattered about on the ground. The trees were windblown and had a lonely look against the sky.

Tim helped Jenna with her backpack. "Do you want me to wait for you to see if everything is all-right?"

"No, no you go on. I talked to Kara last night and she said she would be home all day except for picking someone up this morning. I will be fine. You go and have a great time I will get back to school with Kara next weekend. Thanks for the *buggy ride.*" She gave him a hug then turned toward the path leading to the house.

Tim pulled away and took one last look back. For a moment he had an uneasy feeling about leaving her here by herself – it was a lonely area. By the time he turned onto the highway, he was smiling in anticipation of his week in Carmel; all thoughts of Jenna were gone.

She rang the doorbell and could hear it ringing through the house, soon accompanied by the barking of a dog. A shudder ran through her body. It was as if *someone had walked over her grave.*

The door opened; her feeling intensified. She was looking up into two dark eyes set in a woman's face that looked like it had seen things one would not like to remember.

"Yeah," came from the mouth.

"Hi, I'm Jenna Winslow, Kara's roommate. I have been invi---------"

"Kara no here."

"Well, may I wait for her? When will she be back?"

"No Kara, You go." The door closed.

⋘⋙

Inside the house Kara watched from her bedroom window. She could see Jenna standing on the walkway by the front door. Kara turned to her mother, tears in her eyes.

"Jenna doesn't have a car. Mom, I can't do this to her."

"There's nothing we can do, Kara. Anyway, she is safer this way. If they had let her in she would be in as much trouble as we are. As long as Buddy and his friend are here we can't endanger anyone else. Just pray your father will be back soon with the money and they will leave. Buddy has always been trouble, jail has made him worse. He is more dangerous now than I've ever seen him. We thought he would be locked up for a few more years, and that old woman, Mercedes, is dangerous. I wonder where he found her. She watches us like a hawk and she doesn't like Gracie."

Kara cried softly, "If only the person who dropped Jenna off had waited," She wasn't sure but she thought she had seen the car around campus.

Jenna was stunned; she stared at the house. Tim was gone and it was at least five miles to the village. She backed away from the door, turned and began to walk. She could hardly get lost. This road led to the highway and then north into town. There may be a bus she could get that would take her back to school tomorrow. Tim could have stopped over for something to eat; she might run into him in the village. Her thoughts whirled.

About halfway to the turnoff she saw a car approaching. As it came closer she thought she recognized it. Tim, it was his car – dilapidated, needing paint, but the motor hummed. She waved frantically and the tears started to pour down her cheeks. The car stopping beside her was the best thing she could hope for. "Jenna, what are you doing out here?"

"Me? What are you doing? I thought you would be on your way south by this time, but I did hope you hadn't left yet."

"Get in. My friend is going to be late so I thought I would hang out with you guys for a while." Jenna tossed her bag in the back seat and climbed into the car beside Tim. He never looked so good. "Why are you out here walking alone?"

"Some hideous old lady answered the door and told me Kara wasn't there and to go away."

"Whoa, that doesn't sound right."

"I know. I'm shocked. Kara would never do this to me. She talked to me this afternoon on her cell and said she was going to pick up some woman and then go home. Maybe… that was the woman. It doesn't make sense."

They sat quietly for a moment facing the sea. It was that time of day when the sun slowly slips behind the horizon. The color of the ocean was so intense one would expect the water to boil as it took in the orange orb. The purples and yellows and red colors of the sky gently faded into a dusky lavender.

"Jenna, let's go back to the house and we will both ask for Kara. Whoever answered before may not have understood. We'll ask to speak to her parents and be insistent."

She was slow to answer, "Okay."

Jenna stood in front of the door once more. This time Tim was with her. Now he would see, she thought. She couldn't be wrong. Something was going on. It was quiet inside the house, no sound, a dim light found its way through the transom above the door. Tim knocked. Immediately there was the sound of a dog barking inside followed by a yelp.

They heard someone approaching. Because of the sand cottages near the ocean usually didn't have carpeting, so footsteps on the floors were easy to hear. The door opened. A dark haired man stood there. He was clean, dressed in jeans and a green polo shirt, boots on his feet. He was no one Jenna remembered ever seeing before. "Can I help you?" he asked.

Shadow Cove Incident

Before either could answer a little tan dog shot out of the house and made for the road.

"Damn, that dog has been nothing but trouble." He turned and spoke to someone inside, "Mercedes! I told you to watch that mutt. Well, good riddance." They saw a woman behind him slinking off.

"But isn't that Kara's dog?" Jenna asked.

"She's not here. It won't go far probably be back soon as it gets hungry. What can I do for you? I'm Kara's Uncle Buddy."

"Well, we came to visit Kara, but if she's not here can you tell us where she is? We won't be in town long and we would hate to miss seeing her," replied Tim.

"She left for a visit with her grandma. Don't see much of each other and the old woman is ailing so it was a good time for Kara to visit her. School out and everything, is that all?

"Are her parents here?" Tim asked.

"Went for dinner. Don't know when they will be back. If that's all--" With that he closed the door.

Jenna and Tim just looked at each other. "He just let that dog go and that is not what Kara told me when I talked to her earlier......... Tim, I guess we can't do anymore. I can catch a bus tomorrow morning in town. It will take me pretty close to school and I can call and see if anyone stayed there over the holidays. I've caught rides back to school from there before. ....Tim, I don't know how to feel...... mad at Kara, or scared for her."

Tim was quiet. They got into the car and started back to town. About a half-mile along they saw the dog lying beside the road. "Stop, Tim." Jenna got out of the car and the dog got up and started to move away, limping into the brush. She talked softly as she moved toward the creature. The animal laid down and let Jenna pick it up. She talked soothingly to the little dog cuddled up in her arms.

"What are we going to do with that?" asked Tim.

"I don't know. Take it into town. This is Kara's dog. I can't just let it go."

"Okay, I guess. We'll think about it. But this really complicates things."

They decided on the way to Shadow Cove to get something to eat and then figure out what to do with the dog, Jenna, and Tim's trip south. He really didn't feel right about leaving her there alone. His friend should be arriving in a few hours, they would have to figure something out..

"Look, a pet grooming shop, over there next to the pharmacy. I bet they could take the dog and get it back to Kara. Everyone knows everyone here, the town is so small." Jenna exclaimed.

"You stay here, Jenna I'll go see," Tim parked and went over to the shop. He didn't go in but wrote something down and returned to the car. "It's closed but there's a veterinarian in town. Maybe he can help us. I'm going to get us some 'burgers and ask if anyone knows where his place is. If not I have his phone number, it was on their Closed sign."

"Okay," the dog licked Jenna's hand. "She's sweet."

"How do you know it's a 'she'?"

"I just know."

Tim found a small café where he bought food and even a small patty for 'she'. He found out the veterinarian was close by so they drove there after they had eaten. It was an old Victorian house halfway up on a side street. The house was dark except for lights in the back. There was a illuminated sign on the lawn that read: Dr. James Carson -DVM. They rang the bell and waited. Someone called through the door.

"We are closed except for emergencies."

"This is one," answered Tim.

"Well, go around to the back door."

They found a walkway that led them to the rear of the residence. A door was open and framed in the doorway was a woman waiting for them. "Come in. What's the problem?" She sounded kind. They asked if the dog could stay there until Kara's family could pick her up. Just then a middle-aged man came in the room.

"I'm Dr. Carson……. Why, you've got Gracie. She's belongs to the Jensen family. What are you doing with her?"

Jenna explained the situation thinking *Gracie, that is who Kara was picking up earlier. What's going on? Gracies a dog?*

"Sure, I can keep her and call them in the morning, maybe I should tonight, they will be worried." He removed her collar and handed it to Jenna.

"I won't see Kara to return it."

"Sorry, I can't be responsible, it has all her tags on it; I would feel terrible if it got lost, besides it's our policy. You can give it to her when you meet up at school. You did say you attended school together?"

"Yes, we do. Was Gracie here earlier? Did Kara pick her up from you this afternoon?" Jenna asked.

"No. She's a healthy little thing. I only see her for checkups although it looks like she is favoring her back left leg. I'll take a look at it."

"Would you know of any other place around here that would require her to be picked up?"

"She looks like she's been groomed fairly recently. Maybe the dog parlor in town."

Jenna nodded. She put the collar in her backpack. They thanked Dr. Carson and left. "Whew," Tim exclaimed. "Now what do we do about you. You are kinda stranded here. What would you like to do?"

"Tim, don't you see? Kara said she was going to pick up Gracie and then go home. I thought Gracie was a woman or girlfriend of hers. That means she is here. Someone at that house is lying or hiding something."

They drove back to town in silence. Tim pulled into the parking lot near the bus depot. Upon going in they found there would be a bus leaving in the morning that would take Jenna into the town near their school. She bought a ticket and went out and sat on a bench in the depot. Tim's friend Kirk should be there shortly.

Another problem was what to do for the night. *Some people slept in the depots on the benches, I guess I could do that* she thought. Soon a dusty old truck with a camper on it pulled into the lot and parked. "That's Kirk now," said Tim. He got up and walked over to the truck. They both were glad to see each other and joked around like college guys do. Tim brought him over and introduced him to Jenna. He was a nice looking young man, tall, blonde hair, with piercing gray eyes After all the greetings were out of the way Tim brought Kirk up to speed. He was interested and seemed willing to stay until the next day so Jenna would not be alone.

◄◄►►

Claire was tired of this town - if you could call it that – just a few buildings with a bus stop. There were some businesses such as the one where she had been lucky to get a job. The homes on the ocean side of the highway were used mostly by vacationers so there was not much going on, it all depended on seasonal business. She walked on to her apartment; it was a sleazy efficiency flat above a bait store on the corner, a block from the pet grooming shop where she worked. She was late getting back after shopping for dinner.

Shadow Cove Incident

Claire wondered if she had done the right thing. Buddy had a bad temper. He was supposed to have gotten in touch with her long ago and she felt something had to be done. Cliff, her husband and Buddy had pulled a robbery and hidden the money. Cliff had the key to a locker and only Buddy knew where it was He gave the key to Cliff in exchange for not being as involved so Buddy got off easier than Cliff. They both needed each other to get the money. Clair was Cliff's insurance, she needed the money to hire a lawyer for an appeal.

She turned into the alley that ran along side Maury's Bait Shop, the entrance to her flat was in back. At the top of the stairs she hesitated, her door, it was partially open.

"Come on in Claire," She stepped back. "It's me, Buddy. Come on in."

Buddy had seen Claire through the window of the grooming shop yesterday when he drove Kara to pick up her dog. Later in the day he had driven back and followed her to see where she was staying. This meeting with Claire would be on his terms.

"Where have you been Buddy? I want to get this over with and get out of here."

"It's all set. I have the expense money to get me there."

"How do I know you won't go off, take the stash and leave Cliff and I stuck?"

"Cliff and I are partners and we have an agreement. Say.....you can come along with me if you want."

"Really, ----okay that's a deal."

"Let's have the key."

"I uh - - don't have it. I sent it to you."

"What! How did you do that?"

"You promise I can go with you?"

"Baby, it will be a pleasure."

"Okay, I put it on the dog's collar with the license tags and taped it up behind. It fit real good."

What a dimwit. "Claire the dog ran away earlier this evening what am I going to do now? He screamed. "Get yourself together and come help me look for her."

Claire went over to the closet to get her jacket. It got cool here in the evenings. She never heard him behind her as she bent over to pick up a flashlight. She was a small boned woman in her mid forties so it was easy to break her neck, just a quick snap; she felt like a fragile bird under his fingers.

<hr />

Two phone calls came into the Jensen home that evening while Buddy was looking for Gracie. One came in on the family phone from Dr. Carter, telling them he had the dog and they could pick her up in the morning. Mercedes, Buddy's friend and the Jensen's guard took the message. The other was on Kara's cell phone that Buddy had taken and left in the boathouse where he had his brother Jim tied up. Jenna's message told Kara what had happened and where she and Tim had left Gracie.

Buddy returned from his search tired and dangerous. Mercedes gave him the message from the vet. He couldn't get out of the house fast enough.

<hr />

Jenna woke up early the next morning; she had an early bus to catch. The guys had been nice and pitched in for a motel room for her; they slept in Kirk's camper. She left one last message on Kara's cell telling her about Gracie and that she had the dog's collar.

Shadow Cove Incident

The bus was a few minutes late leaving giving her time to have breakfast and say good bye to Tim and Kirk. There seemed to be a lot of commotion at the other end of the street that was keeping the bus from arriving on time. She relaxed as they finally pulled out and headed north. She would call someone from the school office to pick her up when she arrived in the little town just east of the campus. Everything along the way would be mostly bus stops and cafes to accommodate the passengers. She leaned back and closed her eyes having no idea what was in store for her.

◄◄►►

There was a crowd gathered in the parking lot talking excitedly. Tim and Kirk went over and Tim asked, "Hey, what's going on?"

"A big man in overalls and what looked like fishing gear said, "It's awful. There's been a shooting at the Vet's office. It looks like one of them is dead and the other has been taken in to Hillsborough to the hospital. The kennel boy discovered them this morning."

"I was there earlier last night," Tim told them. "Everything was fine, we dropped off the Jensen's dog."

"You were there son?" A voice came from behind him. "I'm Officer Patton. Are you Tim Corby and where is Jenna Winslow?" He was a big man with heavy eye brows a stern voice and a strong sense of authority about him..

"Jenna just left on the bus. She is going back to school. Her vacation didn't work out for her here."

The crowd had became anxious "How is Jim and his wife?" One asked. "Yeah what 's going on?" Someone called out. "Are they alive?" The group was growing larger and concern for their fellow neighbors showed. "Tell us something." Then from the rear, "Is it true what we're hearing that they are dead?"

"The officer looked grim. "I'm sorry to say Dr. Carter didn't make it but his wife is holding on. She told us about you Tim so we know you are clear but maybe you can tell us something about this dog you dropped off." He turned to another officer and told him to call ahead and have another patrol meet the bus at the next scheduled stop to pick up Jenna. "Tim, come over here with me." They walked over to Officer Patton's car. He looked at Tim and said, "Tell me about last night."

⋘⋙

That morning Buddy went down to the boathouse to check on his brother, he didn't see any problems. When he got away from here he would call and tell his sister-in-law where her husband was. Everything seemed to be okay, he gave Jim some water. Just as he was leaving he noticed Kara's cell and saw there were messages. It was Jenna's calls about the dog and collar, but he already knew that. He smiled. Everything would be fine. "It won't be too long now I will be off and you will be rid of me. I'll have so much money no one will be able to touch me. So long bro."

Now to get her before she gets on that bus, take the backpack and she will think she lost it or it was stolen. I'll take the collar out and just dump the bag. He turned the car north, when he reached the highway about two miles later he saw a bus pull out of the depot – if you could call it a depot, just a small spot in the main shopping area - going north. *Was that the one he wanted?* It had to be. There was only one bus daily each way. His plan now was to pass them and pull into the next rest spot and confront Jenna.

Shadow Cove Incident

◄◄►►

Buddy never did pass the bus it pulled into the rest spot a few minutes ahead of him. He parked and saw Jenna with some of the other passengers. It looked like they were heading for a snack bar close by. He called out as he approached her. "Jenna, wait up a minute. It's Buddy, Kara's Uncle, remember me? You stopped at the house last night."

"Oh! Mr. Jensen. What are you doing here?"

"Kara came home and sent me to get you. She got your voice mail this morning and was upset she had missed you. I can take you back and the two of you can finish your week together."

"I don't know I paid for my ticket and told Tim this was what I was going to do. I'm not sure I should."

"Oh come on. He won't care, he'll be glad you are having fun. You'll have a good time and then go back to school with Kara at the end of the week."

"Well----- Okay I guess so. Wait until I get my things out of the bus and let the driver know I won't be going on with him."

Everything was going his way now, just get that key he thought as he got Jenna situated in his car. Then two Highway Patrol cars pulled into the lot. Buddy thought things had been going too well. One of the officers walked over to them. He was looking at Jenna.

"What's your name young lady?"

"Jenna Winslow, what's wrong?"

"We need to talk to you. There's been an incident and you may have been a witness. Where are you headed right now?"

"Back down to Shadow Cove. Mr. Jensen is taking me to his niece's house to stay for the rest of the week. What kinda incident?"

"We'll talk about it when we get down to Shadow Cove. A police officer will be over to see you at the Jensen's. You go on for now but stay there at the house. We'll be following behind your car Mr. Jensen."

"Oh, I will. I don't have the money to go anywhere else," Jenna replied.

Buddy pulled out of the rest spot and turned south on the road heading to Shadow Cove. The sight of the majestic trees on one side of the highway and the rough cliffs dropping off into the roaring sea was breathtaking. Jenna was quiet not knowing what to think, so much had happened in the last twenty-four hours she let herself relax and watched the scenery. Buddy saw the Highway Patrol cars following them in his rear view mirror a little more than half a mile behind.

The road was tricky and Buddy was very intent on his driving. A curve was coming up ahead in about 200 feet. He made the sharp turn and with some slick maneuvering slid into a copse of trees hiding the car from the highway on the ocean side. One of those places where the trees may have migrated many years ago along the sea side of the cliffs or a barren spot was carved out when travelers settling the missions made their pathway along the coast.

Jenna panicked. "What's wrong?"

"Shut up, give me the dog's collar. You have it in your bag. Be quick."

"What! Do you mean Gracie's collar? Why do you want that?" Through the trees they both saw the officers pass them, her heart dropped.

He pulled out a gun and hit Jenna on the side of her head she slumped over unconscious. Buddy located the collar but no key attached just tape dangling from it. He searched around in her backpack, found the key and put it into his pocket. He got out of the car and went around to the passenger side, pulled Jenna out and shoved her over into the bushes. He didn't bother to see if she was alive.

He knew it wouldn't be long before the police realized he was no longer in front of them and doubled back. He had to get out of here fast. Getting back in his seat he turned the car around, and tossed her backpack onto the side of the road across from where she lay.

He had an idea of how to get out of this mess. There would be a roadblock somewhere up ahead and the highway patrol would be coming south. Soon all the stations would be notified that his car had not shown up at Shadow Cove with Jenna.

Further along there was a spot to pull over to look at the view. He remembered seeing that some of the railings were broken. If he could send the car over the cliff down in to the sea no one would look for him and he could get away. A body wouldn't be found among the rocks and swirling ocean. He would hide in the forest on the other side of the highway and when things cooled down he would hitch hike on up the coast. It would not be easy but for all that money he felt it was worth it. He would wait it out.

"Tim, we were told not to leave and here we are acting like fugitives." Tim and Kirk were driving north to find Jenna.

"I couldn't just sit down there and wait. Something is wrong They could have broken down or something. Buddy Jensen should have been back by now. He ditched the officers. So something isn't right. Maybe we can find them."

"Okay but it looks like this week is a wash," Kirk was disappointed. It seemed like they had driven for miles too upset to notice the beauty around them; the greenery forming a canopy above and the turquoise blue of the sea. Mists floated from the ocean among the trees moving all the time not lying still but swirling through the landscape.

"Hey! What's that on the side of the road? It looks like someone's backpack, pink, a girls," Kirk remarked excitedly.

"I can't stop here, too narrow but if I can go on farther maybe I can turn around and we can double back." Tim found a wider spot in the road farther on and was able to retrace his movements and parked in the copse of trees where Buddy had stopped and dumped Jenna. They got out and Tim crossed the road and retrieved the backpack. "This is Jenna's. Where is she?"

Kirk was poking around in the bushes and weeds along the ledge of the cliff. He saw a shoe protruding from under a dense group of small pines. "Tim, come here I think I found her, but she's hurt, unconscious."

Seeing how close to the edge she was they were almost afraid to touch her. One false move and she could go over or the ground could give way considering how precarious the trees were hanging on.

"Just don't move Jenna, and we will pull you out," Tim warned in case she could hear him. "Don't move." They eased her towards them. Carefully she was put in the back seat of Tim's car. She had a nasty cut on the side of her head and she was sliding in and out of consciousness. The car was headed back to Shadow Cove and that is where they went.

◄◄►►

Buddy pulled into the view spot and it was just as he had remembered. It shouldn't be too hard to knock down the railings and push the car over the cliff. He parked where it would look - in the event someone came by – like a tourist enjoying the view. He took a sledgehammer out of the trunk and found it was harder going than he had anticipated. The railings were metal as well as the posts and they were set in concrete. Some of the footings on the ocean side of the cliff were exposed from erosion.

He finally had an opening large enough to fit the car through. He moved it forward between the posts. Returning the sledgehammer to the trunk, he took out what he thought he would need to endure living in the open for a few nights, could be with luck it wouldn't be that long.

Buddy got back in the car, and left the door open. *Now to turn on the ignition, step on the gas, and jump out.* He had made one mistake; he hadn't calculated enough room needed for the car to go through the space with the door partially open. So as it passed between the posts the door was pushed back pinning him to the car. The earth beneath the death vehicle began to crumble. Then over and over the auto tumbled and when it was soaring through the air the door swung forward with the weight of the man and he was flung out into space, spinning until his body was stopped in its flight pierced through by a sharp pillar of rock at the base of the cliff. He hung there while life slipped away and his blood flowed into the surf, turning it crimson.

※

Claire's death was linked to Buddy when the sheriffs found a journal written by her describing the robbery and Cliff and Buddy's participation in it. It gave all the details the police needed to lead them to search Buddy's room at his brother's house and find enough evidence to locate the stolen funds. Mrs. Carter was able to identify Buddy from a picture of the Jensen's.

Mercedes slipped away when she heard of Dr. Carter's murder. She was never found and probably guessed what Buddy had done so she left. Kara's father was in bad shape when he was finally located. No one went down to the boathouse until the caretaker made his weekly rounds. Jim Jensen was taken to the same hospital where Jenna was being treated. He was suffering from dehydration and mal-nutrition.

A few weeks later back at school Kara and Jenna were celebrities, telling their adventures over and over. Jenna was recovering from a concussion and emotional stress. Though exhausted, she was getting settled in their room sorting out the things she wanted to go in her locker.

Kara, who was helping her came to the door and said, "Hey Jenna, you know that key you kept in your backpack for your hall locker?"

"Yeah, what about it?"

"Well, it's not your locker key."

THE END

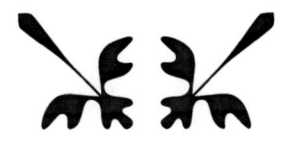

Joseph Bareille

JOSEPH BAREILLE

I'm on the floor looking through a maze of swirling fog, streams of color blurring into each other. There's a sharp pain in my stomach. *What has happened to me?* The room's tilting and everything's getting fuzzy.........

I'm conscious again. I can see my surroundings. I'm on the floor wedged between the counter and a stack of boxes. Looking up at the ceiling, I can see the banner for our weekend sale. It's moving back and forth, the air conditioning must have come on causing the movement. It's making me feel sick watching it.

I have to get up. Got to get up, get some help. I tried and the pain knocked me back to the floor. *How did I get here?* I tried to think. The last I remembered I had been in the stock room when I heard a noise up front. Business had been slow; it seemed like a good time to get started on inventory. I had been about to close, it was almost seven o'clock, and I had sent Marty home earlier, so I was alone. I went up front and saw a man in a grey jacket and black baseball cap standing near the counter by the cash register. I greeted him and asked if I could help.

"Man, give me the money."

I just stared, I wasn't sure I had heard right. I could feel my heart drop. No trouble, I didn't want any trouble.

"The money, man."

I looked over the counter and saw a gun pointed at me. Looking into his face, I was shocked to see a boy about thirteen, tall, slender and nervous. It could have been me when I was about that age, getting into trouble. We didn't have guns; just our hands in our pockets thrust forward.

"Son, you don't want to do this."

"Yes, I do. Give it. Now!"

I tried to remember more but it wouldn't come. Now I'm here on the floor. I looked up and saw that the drawer of the register was open so I guess he got what he wanted. But me, did he use that gun? I tried to look but I couldn't lift my head. I moved my hand down and felt where the pain was bad. It felt wet and I was afraid to feel any farther. Bringing my hand up, I saw red. *Blood. He had used the gun.*

Was this it? Am I dying? How do you know? I felt the panic rise up in my throat, a dry feeling making it hard to swallow. My heart began beating like it was going to burst out of my chest, if it didn't shatter first. *Stay calm Joe, or the blood will pump out faster. I will lose more if I panic. Breathe deep and pray.*

I would have a long wait. The store opened at 9:00 a.m. tomorrow. Rosa would be in after her morning run. My wife, Rosa, what a beautiful woman, in spirit as well as looks. I had been lucky when I found her and she agreed to spend her life with me. She knew I often spent the night on the cot in the office during inventory so she wouldn't worry when I didn't come home.

I think I have been drifting in and out of consciousness for hours. *Wait! There's a woman over there. Who is she? So familiar* - she was silently scrubbing the floor. The swirls of soap went round and round on the marble, forming wet patterns of bubbles. If I tried hard I would be able to reach out and touch them. *It's my mother. Mamma,..... mamma help me. I'm hurt!* ...She was gone. *I must be hallucinating.*

I gave her a bad time when I was young. It couldn't have been easy for her. Dad died when I was six. She had my sisters, Tina and Maria to feed, and me. I got involved with bad company when I was twelve. I was arrested for some petty crimes during the next few years. Mama tried to get me straightened out. Sent me to the nuns at St. Scholastica's School. I did okay for a while then got picked up for stealing a car at fifteen. I was in a Juvenile Detention Home for eighteen months. I didn't do the actual driving but helped on the entry.

Mama supported us by cleaning office buildings, sometimes all night. She was always there to see us off in the morning. My mom, she would be so proud. If she had lived, she would have seen me get an education and go on to open three convenience markets.

During my incarceration, I was turned onto books. I went on to finish high school and then to night school. That's where I met Rosa. She was a teacher's assistant there. *Such a wonderful wife - so happy together - Can't think anymore, I feel sick, I need to sleep . . . .*

◂◂▸▸

Rosa awoke with a start. Was that Joe coming in? She called out, "Is that you, Joe? No answer. It must have been the dream that woke her. She had fallen asleep while reading her book. Joe was working late again tonight. He had been staying at the store for the past three nights. She had hoped for an evening together, maybe dinner or a movie. He was a good man, Joseph Bareille. He always did right by his family.

Maybe she would fix a snack for him and take it to the store. Yes, she would do that. He never ate right when he stayed late. He just grabbed something off the shelf, chips or cookies. They didn't have a deli in the store ... maybe next year. First, she would call so they wouldn't pass each other on the way.

She dialed the number. Busy signal. Who was he talking to at this hour? Maybe he called his sister, checking to see if she was all right. Lazy bum she married; never was any good. Joe helped her out whenever he could.

Rosa put the kettle on for coffee. She got the sliced ham and cheese out of the fridge. He liked mustard on the cheese side and mayo with the ham.

Waiting for the water to boil, Rosa leaned against the counter and thought back to the time when she first saw Joseph. When he walked into the classroom that night she noticed he was nervous, she went over to him to see if he needed any assistance.

When Rosa looked into his eyes she knew he was a good man; a man a woman could trust her life with. Everything was there in those soft brown eyes. It was like she was looking into her future. She knew right then and there they were going to mean something dear to each other.

The kettle whistled, she poured the water into the coffee maker. Finishing the sandwich, Rosa filled the thermos, picked up her keys and purse and left the apartment. It was cold out; luckily she kept a sweater in her car. Putting the car in reverse, she backed out of the garage.

There had been a light rain, just enough to make the streets slick. The store wasn't far, about three miles. Due to the late hour there was little traffic except for a bus. This enabled her to make the trip in good time. She heard the usual street sounds - sirens, the hum of traffic in the distance and tonight the hiss of her tires on the wet pavement.

She saw lights up ahead in the next block - quite a few. The wet surface of the pavement made the reflection of the lights seem more intense. As she drove closer it looked like the activity was in front of the store. *Were those emergency vehicles?* Yes, they were.

The store lights were blazing. Her heart began to beat fast. An ambulance was parked out front, police cars all around, and officers everywhere. *Joe, was he all right?* She came to a halt in the middle of the street and got out of the car on a run. As she neared the store she heard someone call her name. "Mrs. Bareille, Mrs. Bareille." She looked up and saw Marty. He was a young man who lived in the neighborhood and worked part-time in their store. Her heart was pumping hard.

"Marty, what's going on, the ambulance and the police?" Rosa was about to panic she was shaking all over.

"Mrs. Barreile, I'm sorry!"

Rosa went cold. *He's sorry. What is he sorry about?* "Just tell me what happened, Marty."

"Well, Joe sent me home early. Later I was on my way to the bus stop and I passed the store. The lights were still on and the closed sign was not in the window. I wanted to talk to Joe about something so I went in. I'm so sorry, Mrs. Barreile! I called 911. I'm so sorry!"

"What? What are you sorry about" Tell me Marty." He just stood looking at her. She couldn't stand there; she turned and ran towards the store.

"Wait a minute, lady. You can't go in there." It was an officer.

"Yes I can. My husband should be in there. We own the place."

"No! No! Not just now. Wait over there to the side, please."

"What's wrong? Is he all right, Joe my husband? Where is he?"

Someone called from the building, "Charlie, has Winters got here yet?" The officer's attention was diverted for a second. Rosa broke away and ran for the open door. When she entered the building she saw a group of people at the back of the store around the counter.

As Rosa neared them she saw medical attendants, and police officers made up the group. One of the officers was using the phone. There was a stretcher sitting there. *Someone was hurt or sick, that was why the ambulance was outside. Not Joe! It couldn't be him, maybe a customer. Mrs. Chen had a heart attack last month right there in front of the store on the sidewalk. The ambulance and police came then. Yes, that was probably it. Where was Joe? What if something was wrong with him?*

She wasn't thinking straight. Her body felt like lead. Everything had to be all right. She had just been with him earlier that day. They had made plans for the weekend. There was so much ahead of them to enjoy together. He had to be okay. The sickness that she felt inside began to consume her and wash through her being.

The few seconds that it took to cover the distance to the counter seemed to take forever. When she got there she saw a figure lying on the floor. There was so much blood. It was Joe; he was lying in all that blood. *Someone should clean him up. Get him off the floor.* "Somebody, do something. Help him!" The group was gathered around him - she pushed them aside and dropped to her knees beside her husband. No one tried to stop her. There was a man also kneeling beside Joe. He was dressed in white.

"Joe! Joe! What happened? It's Rosa. Honey, what happened?"

"He can't speak ma'am. He's been shot. Let us take care of the situation." It was one of the officers standing there who spoke. Then someone knelt beside her. She felt an arm go around her shoulders.

"Joe, please open your eyes. It's me, honey." He just lay there, pale, so still. She took his hand in hers and held it tight. The tears were streaming down her face. She became aware of strong hands on her shoulders trying to lift her away from her love who second by second, was slipping away from her. She felt a faint squeeze of Joe's hand in hers. He opened his eyes and looked up at her. She saw those same soft brown eyes that she had seen that night so long ago make contact with her and then slowly close. The little bit of life that was left in him slipped away and was lost in the intensity of the moment as he left this earth. They both felt the bond that held them together, drift away, to release each one from the other.

ANOTHER TIME

Another Time

In the darkness of the garage, someone watched. Lighting was placed at each exit and the center of the structure over the elevator and stairwell. It had been raining most of the day and the aisles were wet from the tires of the automobiles. Puddles reflected mirror images caused by headlights from cars passing through the aisles.

Standing behind a pillar, the Watcher had a clear view of the elevator and stairwell. The Watcher stayed in the shadows, alert, slipping back into the darkness when headlights illuminated the surrounding space.

The elevators had opened many times in the past hour signaling tense moments for the Watcher. Once again, the elevator came to life, and as before, the Watcher tensed as it descended from an upper floor. Moving swiftly forward the figure slid a slender silvery instrument from a sheath beneath a heavy coat. A sound from the stairwell made the Watcher freeze.

Emerging from the doorway was a small group of people. Their voices seemed shrill against the echoing silence of the garage. Concealing the stiletto, pulling a hat low, the Watcher turned facing the opposite wall, appearing to be searching for something in the pockets of the coat, presumably keys. The group walked to the other end of the garage, backed their car out into the aisle and disappeared down the ramp.

'It had to be soon; time was running out. Someone was sure to see the figure loitering around the cars' The elevator was again active, the doors opened upon a tall middle-aged man. He carried a brown briefcase and walked toward the cars at the end of the second row.

All of the Watcher's senses were aware of each step the man took. Approaching a dark grey car, the subject put a key in the lock and was about to open the door when he hesitated seeming to remember something forgotten. He turned to retrace his steps.

The Watcher thought, *'I must be sure; yes the license plate was right.'* The Watcher became a predator at that moment, moving forward between the cars about to make a fatal assault. The figure advanced on the prey when the flash of headlights at the entrance of the up ramp caught the Predator's attention.

A van came down the aisle and stopped behind the grey car. Someone inside called out to the man with the briefcase. "Evening, Mr. Charles. It's pretty wet out there tonight, 'been raining all day. We're having some trouble with flooding on the ground level. They've just finished pumping. I'll see you out, if you'd like."

"Thanks Tony. Nice to have maintenance be so helpful." He decided against returning to his office. "I'll follow you."

The Predator had dropped to the floor and rolled under a car, heart beating fast. *'Charles had to be eliminated; he was part of an organization dangerous to the country.'* The dark grey car backed out of the parking space and followed the maintenance van to the down ramp. The Predator crawled out from under the car, stood, then melted into the darkness, vowing,

'Another Time!'

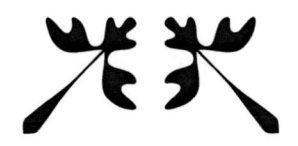

ONE SPRING AFTERNOON

ONE SPRING AFTERNOON

Beth was on top of the world, school vacation a week off, a great feeling about her finals and a good chance she would get the family car on her birthday. That depended on her Dad buying a new one for the family. She already had a learner's permit and drove their pickup around the farm. Beth was a sturdy girl, respectful and studious. She had her mother's black curly hair, a clear complexion and brown eyes like her father. She loved the animals around the farm especially Mrs. Dooley, who was her cat, and Soldier their horse. She always gave them extra treats and they counted on her.

Crossing the street from school, Beth started home. It was a mile if she kept to the roads, but going through the woods cut the distance in half. Glenside was surrounded by timberland, besides it was nice to walk among the trees. Today she decided to take the shortcut through the woods.

She walked slowly, the leaves cushioning her footsteps - some still showed color from last autumn, hidden for a while by the winter snows. Now with spring here and summer ahead, picnics, swimming, hiking, camping and maybe driving her new car (well, new to her), life couldn't get much better. These woods had always been a refuge for her. The canopy of green overhead seemed to gather around and be her safe place. She had been born in the farmhouse that lay on the north side of the creek; it had been the family home for several generations.

Seeing a patch of violets nestled between young saplings, she stopped to pick some and visualized how nice they would be on the window-sill in her bedroom. These were only one of many treasures found here. Green seedlings were bursting into life among the rocks and around the trees bringing spring color everywhere. The shafts of sun glistened on dewdrops where it filtered through the branches, making them look like diamonds nestling among the new foliage. The woods were quiet today, she did not hear birds or see any animal life, she would usually see a squirrel scampering overhead. Today it seemed different. Beth stopped, sensing she may not be alone. She kept very still and listened. Nothing. All was quiet. Silly, her imagination again, the woods would not hold anything sinister. This was her sanctuary.

Moving farther on the path she distinctly heard a noise like a fallen branch being snapped. The sound came from up ahead among the trees to the right. Stopping, her heart thumping in her chest, she stood quietly with all her senses alert, watching and listening. There it was again, a soft crackling sound. She had not been wrong she had heard something. Was it a deer? Or was it just a rotted branch falling in the forest?

It was then that she saw a shadowy figure emerging some distance in front of her. It passed through the trees giving the impression of stealth. She didn't think it was a deer though many lived in this area. No, something about it was human - deer did not wear clothes - it looked like this creature wore blue denim. Watching the figure fading into the distance it seemed like it was carrying something heavy and bulky, staggering occasionally under the weight. Waiting until it was out of sight, Beth continued on the path to the creek moving somewhat faster than her usual pace.

She started to move more quickly, almost running, then running hard, splashing across the creek. Within minutes she emerged at the bottom of the fallow field to the right of her house. The barn was close; out of breath she took shelter there. Dropping her backpack, sitting down on a bale of hay she tried to catch her breath, aware of the sound of her heart pounding in her ears.

"Beth, is that you?" her mother called from the house. Beth started to answer then a hand was brutally clapped over her mouth. She felt something sharp being pressed into her right side. She was pulled to her feet, she drew in her breath, her mouth went dry, and she started to sway. Her legs were giving out. A paralyzing grip of fear attacked her insides. She felt like she was melting and could not stop. Then the shaking started.

"Stand up, or I'll shove this in deeper." She was pulled farther into the darkness of the barn. Shoved to the ground behind the car she had been so eager to have, thinking it would make her world so perfect. It did not seem so important now. All she wanted was for this nightmare to be over. Her mother called out again, at the same time she heard a car pull into the yard.

Susan was on the porch of the farmhouse and was sure she had seen Beth cross the field and go into the barn. Now the sheriff was pulling into the yard. "Hi, Jim, what brings you out here?"

"Hey Susan." He got out of the patrol car and walked over to the porch. Lowering his voice he asked, "Have you seen any strangers out here today?"

"No not for a while. Why?"

"We were transporting two prisoners to the county jail when an accident occurred. They escaped. We are afraid they're in this part of the countryside. I'm tell'in folks that live out a'ways to be careful. Stay inside for a while, keep doors locked."

Horrified Susan looked at Jim then called out frantically. "Beth, where are you? Answer me!" Lowering her voice she turned to Jim. "Just before you pulled in I was sure I saw Beth run into the barn. I called out to her but she didn't answer."

"Wait here. Let me check it out."

"No way, I'm coming."

Beth could see her mother and the sheriff walking to the barn. She was scared for all of them. "Don't move or make a sound or you won't be the only body left in here," the man threatened.

Susan and Jim hesitated just at the barn door. It seemed to Susan that Jim spoke a little louder than usual. "Looks like she's not here. We can wait on the porch. I sure could use some of your good coffee right now. Maybe she left again for a friend's house. You just didn't see her go. School's almost over and kids get antsy lookin' for the fun to start. She'll turn up. Let's get that java." He took Susan by the elbow and led her away toward the house.

Jim had been a friend for many years. He was sixty-one, lean, average height. He never remarried when he lost his wife seven years ago. He was well liked and respected in the area. Susan sighed and let him lead her back to the house. "All

One Spring Afternoon

right, stay for some coffee. I made a pie earlier. Would you like some?" she offered. They were about to go up onto the porch when Jim said, "I've got to check my radio for calls, then you can bring on the feast." Looking grim Jim walked to the patrol car. He had noticed blood and a backpack lying just to the left inside the barn. It was in the shadows so he hoped Susan hadn't seen it. He put a call into the station.

Susan, a tall slim woman with short hair, skin clean and smelling from soap, was a good wife and mother. She and her husband, Chuck had wanted a house full of children but Beth was the only one they were blessed with. Beth meant the world to both of them. To lose her was unthinkable. Seeing the backpack lying there in the barn and Beth not answering left her cold and shaky. She knew what Jim was trying to do. She thought it best to just go along with him. He didn't need to take care of her too, not now. Her hands were shaking when she returned to the porch - coffee and pie on a tray. Jim was sitting on the steps. She sat down beside him. "Did you get through?" She paused. "I saw it too Jim."

"Yeah, try to act casual and smile. Better yet, go in the house and lock the doors?"

"How long?" Susan was desperate.

"Go inside Susan."

"I have to be here."

"No, go now, I mean it."

They heard a noise to their right. It was Chuck coming in from the fields. He was a pleasant looking man, tall, tan and muscular from working the farm. "Hi Jim. I see you are eating some of my wife's famous pies. I'll take care of Soldier and then join you." Chuck slid down from the horse and turned toward the barn to put Soldier in his stall.

"Chuck, wait a minute, before you do that, I need to talk to you." Jim told him the situation, Chuck's face showed his shock.

"What are you doing sitting here eating? Let's do something."

"We are. Men are on their way, State Troopers and our guys. We can't take any chances. Trust me for now." They sat there for what seemed like eternity, when Susan felt that the landscape seemed to be alive. No one was in sight. It was only a feeling of unseen presences.

◂◂▸▸

"I don't want to hurt you kid, this will be over as soon as we can get away. Where is the key to the car?"

We? Beth thought, "*He's taking me with him?* "I don't know, I'm too young for a car. I won't be sixteen for another month." He seemed to think it over and realized she might be telling the truth. He shoved a dirty rag into her mouth.

"You better not be lying. It could get mighty rough for you," she was warned.

The rag, tasting of dust and oil, gagged her. Then Beth heard a groan, someone else was in the barn with them. He pushed her to the ground, tied her with a piece of rope her dad used for towing. She was dragged across the floor and left in Soldier's stall. Beth heard him talking in a hushed voice to someone. "*Two of them! Maybe he wasn't going to take her with him after all.*" It was hard not to cry. She choked back her sobs. Oh, why hadn't she gone straight to the house instead of in here? Who were they?

◂◂▸▸

One Spring Afternoon

Unknown to Beth's parents and the sheriff, a hornet from a nest in one of the oak trees was flying around Soldier. Snorting, he flicked his tail and moved nervously.

"Whoa boy!" Chuck exclaimed. "He needs water and his feed. It was a hard day in the fields." Just then the hornet attacked, sinking his stinger into Soldier's left hindquarter causing the horse to rear up and tear off for the barn with Chuck running behind him. The men hiding inside were horrified by the large fierce monster, glazed red eyes bulging, flared nostrils shooting smoke and fiery wrath entering the barn bearing down on them, surely intent only on their destruction.

Outside officers came from everywhere, the back of the barn, the sides with Chuck and Jim in front. The escapees were so frightened by Soldier they did not put up much of a fight and were soon both in custody.

Where was Beth? They heard Soldier whinny, he was standing in front of his stall, snorting and pawing the ground. Susan who had followed Jim and Chuck ran over to the horse. She saw Beth lying on the floor of the stall. "Here she is" called Susan. "Are you all right honey? I was so worried. Thank God we found you." Chuck ran over, untied Beth and hugged her tight to his chest. "We saw some blood near your backpack", Susan told her.

"The blood belonged to one of the men. He was hurt. I'm scared Mom. I want to get out of here, please." Chuck lifted Beth into his arms and carried her to the house. They realized how close their life came to being changed drastically in a few hours. Beth was fine physically but emotionally the teenager had an experience that she would not forget anytime soon.

Soldier was given an extra bit of oats that evening and Susan was happy her family was safe. It was a while before Beth went to the barn again. Mrs. Dooley had kittens in the barn that spring. It was impossible for Beth to stay away from them for too long. Anyone passing through Glenside may see a young black haired girl proudly driving along the country road in her almost new car.

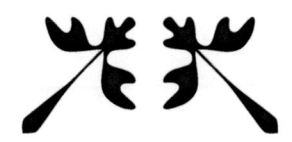

Legacy

LEGACY

As the express pulled out of the station Cindy Vlad Wychick felt a thrill of satisfaction for what she had just accomplished. This was once her home and her fortune was largely due to her famous great Uncle Vlad. So she had returned six months ago to invest some of the money in the restoration of the village.

The old Peonari Castle where her great uncle had lived was lying in ruins. She intended to restore it to its original majesty. The town's income largely depended on tourists the castle attracted.

The buildings were crumbling and soon the decay would have reached deep into the recesses of the mountain where her great uncle had slept. It was in the surrounding villages where the events had begun so long ago that shook the region with fear.

Cindy had come to make a difference. Her peers considered her a philanthropist. She had been actively engaged in restoring artifacts around the world after disasters had damaged them. Cindy had modified her name long ago. The family name had caused too many questions and attention.

As the train reached the outskirts of the village she smiled as she read the sign alongside the tracks.

Jeanne Wray

You are leaving Argus Valley
Site of Castle Peonari
The Former Home of Vlad Dracula
Pop.3500

She leaned back on the cushions in the compartment, closed her eyes and congratulated herself on a job well done.

⋙⋘

The ship soared through space, on a trip that was the answer to a dream of the young dark-haired lad looking out the window into the galaxy. The blackness seemed to go on and on with glistening stars assuring him that he was on his way to Earth.

Nigel was 21, just making the age requirement for the Earth Work Tours. He had been born on Venus - one of the farming planets. His family had been assigned a large bracket of woodlands used for timber. They named the parcel Vlad after his mother's great uncle in Transylvania.

His father, Jacque, had Nigel out among the trees when he was young and the two of them had kept the bracket productive for many years. Nigel liked the darkness of the forest. He never saw much sunlight working among the trees from dawn to dusk almost every day. Now it was time for Nigel to go to Earth and further his education.

Jacque and Cindy, Nigel's mother, had emigrated to Venus from Washington State. Cindy's family was originally from Romania in the Transylvania Mountain area. She had come to the United States and met Jacque on a space voyage to the planets that were available for colonization. They chose Venus because of its close proximity to Earth.

Legacy

The plan was for Nigel to work in the forests of Washington while attending a nearby University. With his experience he was assured of steady part-time work. Civilization on Venus was still too young to have the educational advantages that Earth could offer.

He hoped that maybe a change of scene would stop the dreams that plagued him. He would dream of soaring through the darkened sky until dawn or walking through the underbrush of the forests. Upon waking he always felt shaken, like something had passed that he could not understand. He often awoke to reddish brown stains on his pillow. Cindy told him he had nosebleeds sometimes when he slept. He wondered why she had become excessively vigilant when she found the soiled linens. He did know that many nights she stayed outside his door until dawn.

There was one dream that Nigel tried to forget. Several men and women ran screaming and stumbling in their flight to get away from some unknown menace. He never remembered how that dream ended. He was always exhausted when he woke and the blood stains were on the bed linens.

Suddenly he noticed that the activity in the cabin had changed. Asking an attendant he was told that they were entering Earth's atmosphere, the mother planet where all had begun. Then as quickly as it had started the excitement turned to cold fear.

Something was terribly wrong. The ship began to shake violently and flames could be seen from the windows. She was spiraling downward burning up, the cabin's temperature became extremely intense. The lights failed. Panic enveloped them all. There was nothing to stop the downward path of the ship.

A shadow rose out of the blackness fluttering among the passengers leaving some with a puncture wound near the jugular vein, then going on to the next, gorging itself with the life blood of each panicked victim.

The ship spiraled downward, a blazing object in a black expanse of space until nothing remained but tiny fragments of matter drifting off into the void of the atmosphere. If there had been a witness to the unbelievable destruction, they would have seen what appeared to be a small dark form with webbed wing-like appendages, separate itself from the drifting debris and glide downward into the blackness toward Earth..... *Was this an end of a legend or the beginning of a new one?*

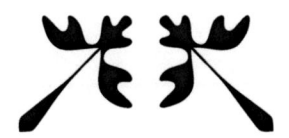

Bessie

BESSIE

Bessie was a large strong woman, yet warm and soft. The color of cocoa with the smell of fresh daisies and cinnamon wafting around her as she quietly moved through the house. Sara loved her; they spent many days together. Bessie was the maid for Sara's Aunt.

Sara lived in Newark, New Jersey with her parents but traveled once a month to see her doctors at Children's Hospital in Pittsburgh. During her visits she stayed with her Aunt and Uncle on their farm in Glenshaw, Pennsylvania. She enjoyed the farm so was allowed to stay on longer than her visit required. Sara was now about four years old and had been making these trips for several years. She had polio at seventeen months old so these visits were necessary.

The two of them were friends. Bessie was always baking cookies, cakes, and doughnuts, candy all those good things we love. The little girl would always lick the frosting bowls and Bessie would sometimes give her a little extra. Sara spent most of her days with Bessie who always had time for her.

One rainy day Sara's Aunt reluctantly drove into town on business. Bessie and Sara were alone that day when the storm swept across the land with a fury.

The afternoon turned into night. Thunder roared across the skies and the bolts of lightning seemed to flash through the windows and the world seemed to hang in space and shiver. Sara was frightened and clung tightly to Bessie. She held her on her lap during those dark moments giving her the hope of a rainbow when the storm was over.

They were sitting there, Bessie telling Sara stories about her childhood and Sara with big eyes, hearing the horrific sounds of the storm battering the house. Suddenly a blazing blue light illuminated the room for what seemed like a never ending pause in time then a sharp cracking sound, followed by a loud crash. The entire house shuddered. Movement could be felt everywhere.

Upon checking the house Bessie found that a large oak had almost split in half outside in the garden and the upper portion had landed in the attic. They were safe. The lower floors were not damaged and no fire. Bessie contacted Sara's Uncle at his office. She held Sara in her lap until her Aunt and Uncle arrived. That day was burnt into Sara's memory forever.

Sara spent many happy times with Bessie through the following years. Then on one of her visits Bessie was gone. Someone else was working in her place. Sara was very sad and did not understand. *Bessie would not have left me without saying goodbye. Something terrible had happened to her. She was dead!* Sara thought. No one would tell her anything except that Bessie had gone to help her family. The new maid was nice but it was not the same. She still continued to visit her Aunt and Uncle but not as often because she no longer needed to see her Doctors each month.

It was some years later that Sara heard the true story. Bessie had every other Thursday and alternate Sundays off. She had an apartment in town near her family. It was on one of her days off that she discovered all the money she had been saving for years was gone. The only one who would have had access to the funds was her boyfriend. She confronted him,

BESSIE

they argued and he walked out. Bessie followed him down to the street taking with her a knife from the kitchen. She walked up behind him and stabbed him in the back.

She was arrested and went to jail. Her boyfriend lived. When she was sentenced Sara's Aunt appeared before the Court as a character witness. Later when Bessie was eligible for parole her Aunt was able to have her released to her. When Bessie's probation ended she stayed on at the farm for several more years and then went back to her old neighborhood. Sadly she later was returned to prison for shooting a boyfriend. This one did not live. Bessie died in prison.

*This is a true story only the names have been changed.

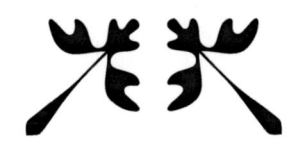

End Of A Journey

END OF A JOURNEY

I was weightlessly floating, floating gently, soaring along in the azure blue skies. My cloud suddenly dropped out from under me with a jolt. Opening my eyes, I found myself on the cabin floor, everything was black, the noises were deafening. I shook my head trying to clear it and make some sense of what I was experiencing. Light suddenly flooded the room. Francis stood there framed in the doorway.

"Isabella! Isabella, are you and the children all right?" Just then I realized that my babies were crying in the background and the ship was shuddering and listing to one side.

"What happened?"

"I'm afraid there's a problem. Hurry, get dressed, you and the children, pack just the necessities those we planned in the event of a quick disembarkation. I will return shortly. Just do what I say, and quickly. Your lifejackets! Don't forget your lifejackets." He was gone as if in a dream.

We couldn't be leaving the ship, it couldn't sink. Not the Titanic. Francis was one of the engineers that worked on the plans. He had said that it was a break-through - unsinkable. Trying to keep my heart from pounding and my head from whirling, I realized I had to get hold of myself. Charlie, our three year-old and Emma, our 18 month-old were shrieking from the alcove just off our room. I ran to them and saw that they were not hurt, only frightened. I hurriedly dressed, then returned to the babies and dressed them.

By now the cold fear was sinking deeply within my bones. I could hear screams coming from somewhere within the bowels of the ship. Where was Francis? I needed him. Please God save us, send my husband back to us, now. I was just going to take matters into own hands and step into the hall with the children when the door opened and there he was. My heart leaped. Thank you, God!.

Quickly," he ordered, "let's go."

Francis carried Charlie and I took Emma. I started for the gangway to my left but Francis took my arm and led me to the right. There was a strange frenzy and excitement in the hall. I could hear so many voices around me. People were shouting and frantically running back and forth. As Francis guided us through the crowd, I could feel his strength, which I always depended upon. Water was sloshing in my shoes as we proceeded down the hallway. We stopped at a door marked "Personnel Only." He opened the heavy door and pushed us inside.

Down a short narrow hall there was a gangway going up and not as crowded as the area we had just left. We mixed in with the crew, one took Emma from me and we were able to move faster. We kept climbing higher and higher. As we went upward more people joined us. My legs were about to give out when we finally reached the deck. Next, find our Lifeboat Station.

It was then that I heard someone saying, "Woman and Children first." No! We could not be separated. What would I do without him? We had brought two beautiful children into the world; we loved each other. Just then our Station was in front of us. A member of the crew stepped up and said, "Room for three, you and your children lady. Step quickly, many are waiting, you know." I will remember those words as long as I live.

I looked up at my dear husband as he handed Charles down to some one in the lifeboat. So fast! How could this be happening so quickly? I wanted to hold Francis for just a little bit.

Then I felt Emma leaving my arms. I think I screamed. I clung to Francis. He kissed me, and then pushed me down into the hands of others in the lifeboat. I grabbed my children and turned and looked up into my husband's face. No, this was not happening; tears were streaming down his cheeks, his face was contorted with grief. The lifeboat began to move. I kept my eyes on Francis. My heart wrenched as we drifted further and further from the ship.

That was the last time I saw him.

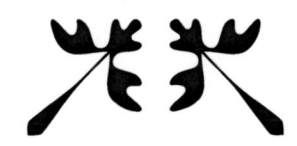

Carla Shannon

Carla Shannon

The coffee flowed across the floor, spreading and dripping into grout depressions, hesitating as if on a precipice spilling over to fill the recess then moving to the next tile on the white ceramic surface - hurrying to meet an advancing reddish brown fluid to join and become one. The thick red wetness drew the coffee in slowly and formed a blended pool surrounding the mound of human flesh on the floor.

◂◂▸▸

Carla had not felt well when she woke that morning. She would have preferred to stay in bed a little longer under her soft warm rose print comforter. Work started at nine a.m. promptly, at the library. A new librarian was to start today and Carla was going to train her in *their* ways. It will be nice to retire next month, to have a lazy day if one wanted. She still intended to do the 'Children's Books' weekly reading. That would take only two hours with set up, the actual story telling, then catching up on all of the library gossip afterward.

Looking into the bathroom mirror only convinced her that she did need a long deserved rest. She was a little pale and there seemed to be a bluish cast around her mouth. Her hair, once almost blue black, was now heavily salt and pepper. Once it was thick and shiny, now thinning so that it just hung limp if she didn't have it properly cut and styled. Nothing could be done about the pull of gravity upon her features. Her clear blue eyes were her best feature and had remained bright not faded, as had so many of her friends. Carla owed her coloring to her Irish heritage.

Her weight was a problem. The doctor had advised her to lose some pounds. She would work on that when she had time after her retirement, maybe early morning walks. She could get a dog that would inspire her to take those walks.

She felt anxious this morning and felt some fluttering in her chest upon rising, probably just anxiety about meeting the new librarian. There had been some lightheadedness yesterday when walking home from work. What did one expect at 72 almost 73. She was healthy all of her life, never married. She had been a good daughter taking care of her mother and father until they went home to be with the Lord. It was an auto accident that took them. Her father was killed instantly and her mother died at the hospital later that day.

Carla went into the kitchen; put the coffee on to brew, took a cantaloupe from the windowsill and set a place at the tiny table in the corner. She used the raffia placemat, nice and proper and her Mother's sterling silver flatware. Carla liked nice things – crossing over to the counter she saw the coffee was almost done - two cups as usual.

She removed a knife from the wooden holder. It was dull – as were all of her knives. Her father had always kept them sharpened, something she never kept up. As she plunged the knife into the melon she felt a dull heavy pain shoot across her chest. She held onto the counter with her left hand. Another wave of pain coursed through her upper body, her knees buckled.

With an awkward movement, she let go of the blade handle, sending the cantaloupe spinning across the counter colliding with the coffee pot, tipping it over. The contents spilled out and trickled down onto the floor.

The melon continued its journey rolling from the counter landing on the floor with enough force to cause one side to smash against the cold hard tile sending the slim handle up into the melon. The tip of the blade pointing upwards like a shining spire held upright by the flattened part of the melon. There was not time for it to roll on its side.

Carla was falling face downward, she didn't see the melon with its pinnacle thrusting upwards. She fell on that spire embracing it with the heavy mass of her body causing it to remain upright piercing her heart. She never felt the knife enter her chest; her heart had stopped before she reached the floor. That was the day Carla Shannon permanently retired from the Shannon City Library.

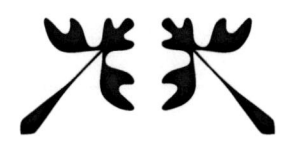

The Arrival

The Arrival

I had been standing at the Naval Air Station in New Jersey watching for the arrival everyone was waiting for. The drive was long so I had left Chicago last evening, I was tired but my excitement was keeping me on my feet.

It was still daylight and the zeppelin was not due to arrive until close to dusk. I was there to meet the ship. My son, Herbert, a passenger on board was coming home for a visit. My name is Audrey O'Laughlin.

A cheer rose from the crowd. It was after 7:00 p.m. in a darkening twilight sky. Looking off into the distance a speck could be seen moving toward us. I stood there and watched the great object come closer to earth. Visibility would soon be a problem as the ship began to descend. It was reported there were 97 on board this time - including crew and passengers.

I saw two landing ropes drop that were to ease her down. These would be tied to cars on the ground. The cars were set on a circular track designed to hold the nose of the ship down at a 30 degree angle helping it jockey into a position for its mooring. They would move along on the track to guide her in.

We had been told , "There was some wind today so everything may not play out as expected. This had been done many times so not to worry." As we watched the ship come nearer it suddenly burst into flames leaving the spectators in hysteria. Screams came from everywhere. "Run for your lives." Those who could did. Two explosions lit up the sky. Passengers sitting close to the windows in the gondolas were vaulted or leaped out on to the ground because of the energy of the force – that jump saved some of their lives.

Me, I was thrown onto my back about 50 feet from where I was standing and slammed into the side of a mechanics shed. When my head cleared, I realized the impossible had happened. On the evening of May 7th, 1937 at Lakehurst, New Jersey, *The Hindenburg* had exploded.

I could not find my son. Not on the ground or in the makeshift infirmary set up in one of the hangars. He could be in one of the back gondolas. I couldn't get near the zeppelin it was burning like fury in hell.

I felt a chill take hold of my heart. Where was he? I had Herb's old bedroom all ready for him. I had prepared foods that he liked. I asked everywhere, no one had seen him. Maybe he had been taken to a hospital and I missed him. Then I thought, I would never see him again. I felt the hot tears starting to swell behind my eyelids. I didn't want him to see me crying if I should come upon him suddenly.

It seemed like hours that I walked around that field. It was about 1:00 am when over a megaphone a Mrs. Audrey O'Laughlin's name was called out. Though they couldn't hear me I screamed, "I'm here."

"Come to the Red Cross Station. Please, Mrs. Audrey O'Laughlin." Well, I ran faster than a greyhound. When I was just about there a man was walking out of the hangar towards me. His face was completely black and his clothes badly burnt.

"Mom?" He asked.

The Arrival

"Herb, is that you?" We fell into each other's arms. I felt such a rush of love and relief like I had never felt before. He was alive. I could take him home.

There had been ten Inter-Continental flights made in 1936 with the Hindenburg. This flight from Germany was the first this year to make the crossing. The distressing news reached Berlin and Frankfort about 2:am on the eighth.

No one knew what had caused this disaster. They were using hydrogen and blue gas which was considered the most dangerous of all gasses for inflation of airships - as their fuel - and in the past seemed to have good luck with it. We Americans had our problems with dirigibles – mostly structural. It was also suggested that commands necessary for the cars were not received by one of the drivers. Whatever happened history was made that day.

Later we knew 34 were dead out of 97 passengers and crew. Many were severely and critically burned and taken to local hospitals. The dirigible was burnt beyond belief. The screams of pain and the smell of burning flesh made a memory never to be forgotten.

Secretary Hull sent the following message to Konstantin von Neurath, the German Minister of Foreign Affairs

" I extend to you and to the people of Germany my profound sympathy at the tragic accident to the dirigible Hindenburg and the resultant loss of life to passengers and crew."

"It is too terrible to believe." Admiral A.B. Cook of Naval Aeronautics wrote.

*Authors note. I lived in Newark, New Jersey during those years and frequently saw the silver dirigibles sailing overhead. Everyone would go outside to view them. When the Hindenburg

blew up I remember the news reports. After that, we did not see as many coasting above us.

Herbert James O'Laughlin was a real passenger on the Hindenburg. In my story I took the liberty of having his mother there at the disaster. She was in Chicago and as soon as he found a phone he called to let her know he was alive.
Ref: New York Times – May 7, 1937 Edition

The Meeting

The Meeting

The woman looked old and fragile, she wore gloves, carried a large shopping bag and walked with a limp. She was dressed shabbily and was unsteady on her feet. The clothes she wore looked as if they had been purchased in many thrift shops throughout the years. Her choice of colors had long faded into soft grays and sepia tones. The glasses she wore - probably bought at a second-hand store - pinched so deeply you could imagine the indentations they left on the bridge of her nose. The hat covering her head made an effort to boast a veil, no hair was visible but the impression was gray. She had a memorable smile, everyone who had noticed her later remarked about her kind face.

She stopped in front of a movie theater and approached the cashier's booth. After buying a ticket she entered the theater. Her manner gave the impression of someone who had taken refuge from an unknown evil on the streets. Hesitating, she looked around. Perhaps she was waiting for her eyes to adjust to the darkness. The theater, not being full, she had her choice of seating but she chose to sit in the back row next to an already occupied one. With a sigh she dropped wearily into it. About halfway through the film she seemed to be sleeping. This was a war movie - the explosions and gunfire were almost continual. The noise did not seem to make it an ideal place for a nap.

After a while she sat up and appeared alert. It wasn't too long after that she leaned over to the man next to her and asked sweetly, "Would you mind keeping my seat? I must step out for a moment."

He looked at her, she reminded him of an old aunt he hadn't seen in a while. "Certainly, go right ahead," he said. '*Sweet old lady,'* he thought, pleased that he could help.

She started to step over his feet when she stumbled, catching herself against his chest with her right hand, her left slipping into the pocket of her shabby coat. Time seemed to stop. There was a moment of hesitation and embarrassed surprise on both their parts. The sound effects from the film were ear splitting at that time. She righted herself and shuffled out to the aisle. As she limped to the exit the man's head slumped forward onto his chest, a dark pool was forming under his seat and running under the row in front of him. Without hesitating the old woman entered the Ladies Room. She was never seen coming out.

A tall mature lady dressed in a black suit with a red scarf at the throat, carrying a black patent leather bag - along with one that didn't seem to belong - exited the cinema through a side door opening onto an alley. The woman made her way behind the buildings where she passed a group of homeless people. She walked to a trashcan. A fire burned inside to provide warmth. Tossing the extra bag into the blaze, she moved on using the alleyway to reach the boulevard then entered a restaurant. She sipped a white wine and ordered dinner.

Before long, a dark man with a heavy beard wearing an open necked shirt and blue jeans joined her. Under the beard his complexion was deeply scarred with pockmarks. He wore

The Meeting

an expensive watch on his wrist and massive gold chains around his neck.

"Is it done?" he asked.

"Yes. This is the last time we meet like this. Next time we will conclude in the usual manner."

"We shall see."

He placed a thick brown manila envelope on the table, nodded, rose and sat at the bar. She ate her dinner then went to the lounge. The lady was never seen coming out.

The arrival of a flight to Denver was delayed due to a passenger being late for boarding. The bearded man was killed instantly on the way to his hotel by a hit and run driver. The man in the theatre was thought to have been shot by an accomplice in a gunrunning scheme. It was a case the ATF had been working on for months. No connection was ever made between the two deaths. A witness said an old lady was behind the wheel in the hit and run case.

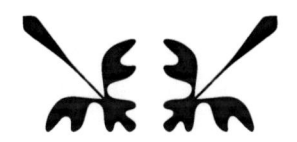

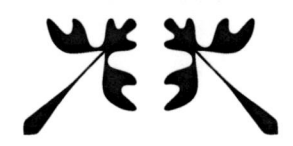

Future/Destiny

FUTURE/DESTINY

When Charles Jamison left for work that morning he had no idea what fate had in store for him. He used the same familiar route that he took everyday driving a bright red convertible always with the top down, unless the weather was foul. Charles was very fond of his car even though his family had gone without many essentials to satisfy his many desires.

He stopped at a coffee shop, which was a ritual for him, ordered an espresso, with a dash of milk - low fat - had to watch the waistline. His clothes were from all the best stores and boasted designer labels. No need to look middle-aged if he could help it. Charles had an eye for the girls. Returning to his car he continued down the street unaware of the death sentence waiting just ahead of him. He entered the intersection of Raleigh and Converse when a semi crossed at the same time from the opposite direction.

◄►

John Merrick had started his day early. He had spent the night in a rest spot about fifty miles north. The delivery John was making was heavy, a little over weight. He was glad there weren't any weigh stations along his route. John was carrying sacks of cement stacked on large wooden skids. He had been having problems with his load shifting on this trip. The bands holding the bags onto the skids were slipping and John had stopped more than once to adjust them. Before he left this morning he had checked everything and was satisfied that they would hold for the few miles he had left to go.

Entering the city that morning John felt good. The money for this trip would finally enable him to make the final payment on the rig. John saw the intersection ahead and prepared to stop if the signal changed. It was a go. He was almost through when the car in front of him braked suddenly to avoid hitting a small dog that dashed into the street. John slammed on his brakes and felt his load shift forward and then snap back. The bands strained. Then behind him he heard the sound of them breaking and the thud of the cement sacks landing on the street. His heart jumped in his chest with the realization that part of his load had fallen into the intersection.

Looking out of his window he saw that some of the bags had split open and the sandy gray matter was spilling onto the pavement. John had seen the red convertible enter the intersection and pass him from the opposite direction. Now looking in his rear view mirror he saw that part of his load had fallen into the red car.

Charles Jamison didn't die immediately. He certainly received a concussion from the weight of the bags, but not enough to kill him. It was the cement that did it. All that was required was water to be added to make it ready for use. The dry mix filled his mouth, eyes and nose. It took some time to clear the heavy bags from the car and then dig him out of the spilled cement; by that time the moisture from his body had started it to set. When they got to him he had suffocated.

It was four o'clock in the afternoon when Carly heard that her Daddy was dead. Carly was eight years old and Charles

Jamison was her father. When she came home from school that afternoon she saw family cars parked in front of her house. When she entered the living room she saw her Mom had been crying. She knew something bad had happened.

Later in her room she hadn't felt bad when she heard that her Daddy was dead. Carly felt guilty because she couldn't cry like the others, she wanted to smile. He never would be coming home again. That meant he couldn't hurt her anymore. Daddy always said he loved her best but she had been afraid to tell him that his love sometimes hurt.

'One man's destiny ... a little girls future'

STORIES TO MUSE OVER

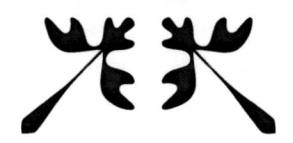

MIRROR REFLECTIONS

When I looked in Grandma's old mirror I saw my image in the glass. It had been a long time since I had been in the attic. The girl I saw all those years ago was young and full of hope. Now what I saw was an old woman with the trials of many past sorrows etched on her face and bent body. I have been packing and planned on moving to a smaller house that is what brought me up here today - to sort things out. It was time to move on.

As I stared and took stock of what time had done to that child a strange thing began to happen. My image in the mirror began to change before my eyes. The years dropped away and the figure reflecting back was the young girl I remembered.

Watching, enthralled at the change, I noticed movement behind her in the mirror. I saw reflections of others. Looking closer my mother and father were sitting at our kitchen table. My brother and sisters were there also along with a young girl they looked so happy; I could see they loved each other. The girl looked familiar. *Was that me? Yes, I knew she was.* She had on that pink dress with the eyelet ruffle around the skirt. I always liked that dress and wore it when I went somewhere special..

I turned around to join them but all I saw behind me were cobwebs, dusty broken furniture and boxes that had been stored there for years. I turned and faced the mirror; they were in there, not behind me. I reached out to touch the surface. My hand did not stop at the glass but slipped into the space beyond. I pulled it back and tried again thinking I was dreaming. Yes! It did go through. I stepped forward slowly and was enveloped into their world.

The familiar girl was gone and I was sitting in her chair wearing the pink dress. A peaceful feeling washed over me. They had all been taken from me in a auto accident long ago. If I only had known, I could have found them here and avoided all the years of loneliness.

I have been living here with my grandmother. She has been gone for a while now. I never married but lived with her since the accident. It is wonderful to be with my family again even if this is a fantasy my brain conjured up. There was magic in that old mirror today, something I will treasure forever.

Downstairs the moving crew had been packing all morning and were finally ready to start on the attic. What they found was not what they expected. The lady who had hired them was lying in front of an antique mirror. She had a smile on her face and looked like she was sleeping but in reality death had taken her into another world.

THE DOOR

I stood in front of the door, reached out and touched the handle. I pulled my hand back it felt as if burning coals had seared it. I knew I had been here before. Sweat poured down my body. I was shaking. Dare I try again? I reached for the handle. My hand would not move. The last time should have been enough. Why was I still standing here? I knew inside there were no walls, just an empty void with black creatures swirling around and around – shapeless and hooded, yellow eyes boring out from under their brows. They never stopped moving but had begun gathering around me – twisting and turning. I ran and fell into emptiness, dropping down, down, maddening sounds all around me. Then here I was standing in front of that door again. No. I turned and walked away.

THE ROSES

The white roses growing along Jimmy's fence had been planted back in the '50's. The plants climbing along the fence in a most pleasing fashion were charming. Thick gnarled vines produced a myriad of beautiful flowers each year. The shiny green leaves sparkled with early morning dew. Looking into the droplets they mirrored the world around you creating a fairylike atmosphere.

The fence ran about fifty yards long across Jimmy's property. One thing very odd about the roses, they grew profusely for about six or seven feet along the fence-line. The rest of the growth was sparse and in some places there were no flowers to be seen. Many of the canes were shriveled and some looked dead. It was a shame that the beautiful blooms did not grow uniformly across the front of the property. One would guess that this was the only place where fertilizer had been raked in.

There was no longer a gardener, no one to feed or properly care for the plants so what was keeping this area so beautiful made one wonder. If Mr. Hoffa had still been around I don't think the rest of the vines would have been in such a sorry state.

Jimmy was last seen leaving the Machus Red Fox restaurant in Bloomfield Township, Michigan - a suburb of Detroit. He was in a car owned by Tony Jack Giacolone, driven by an unknown driver. Jimmy was to meet with two Mafia leaders that day - Tony Jack was one of them. Jimmy Hoffa was never to be seen again. Who knows where he can be now?

There was one other strange thing about the bushes. The roses that were thriving were not completely white. The petals were streaked with pale shades of pink and crimson. It was like rain had showered them with a reddish mist or the ancient roots had gone deep into the earth to discover a new a feeding supply.

My Treasure Box

I gazed at the box in my daughter Michelle's hand. "Where did you find that honey?"

" In Dad's work bench."

"In his work bench?"

"Yes, and Mom he saved things just like I do."

"What do you mean? Let me see."

I had lost track of that box long ago. I had kept all my treasures in it when I was in school. After college it disappeared.

We had buried my husband, Jack, the week before. He died suddenly of a heart attack. Going through his things was hard on all of us. Johnny our son, and Michelle were each helping me. They were looking through the garage and I was going through more personal items.

Michelle handed me the box. When I touched it a shiver went through me, I knew the contents might change my life. It was like touching old times. I had kept many dear souvenirs and precious memories in it. Now I kept them in albums and drawers. With marriage, babies and all things that form a family I had discarded the box after I was married. I had taken my treasures out at the time. I thought it was long gone.

Lifting the lid I held my breath not knowing what I would find. What could Jack have used this for? Tools, maps, what would a man keep in a box like this? There before my eyes were Birthday, Anniversary, and Valentine cards that I had given him through the years. There were theater stubs, a baby's rattle, a dried boutonnière and an old skate key from when he was a boy. These were things that he and I shared during our life together. He kept these and never said a word.

Jack was not a demonstrative man. There were times when I wondered if he still felt anything deep for me - or for all three of us. He seemed to drift away after our son was born. I know there were many demands at his office and I guess I became involved with the children. We didn't seem to have as much time together as we once had.

Now seeing what he treasured of the precious moments of our life my heart cried and soared at the same time. I knew then our marriage had been true. He really cared. I would be able to live the rest of my life knowing that I had been loved. What a wonderful gift he had left me.

A Time Together

I looked down into the water searching, it rippled and stirred from the wind blowing across the lake. Then I found him, he was floating on his back looking so relaxed. He saw me and waved, beckoning to come swim with him.

He was my son a good boy and a promising fine athlete. I considered going for a swim on the way out here - we hadn't swum together in a long time. The air had a chill in it but I wanted to join him. That was the reason I came here today, to enjoy time together.

The water was cold but refreshing as my body slipped into it. I always warmed up after the initial shock. There he was swimming a few feet away. We swam together underwater side-by-side for a while when I became very cold. Maybe if I went to the surface I would warm up a bit. I swam upward but I couldn't find the opening in the ice where I had entered. My body began to feel warm again as I searched, warm enough to swim on.

Where was he? I looked around. There, over there. I swam to him and we went on together.

The Flight

Icy fingers of fear raced along my spine when I felt his eyes on me. I didn't look up just prayed. Senses reeling I tried to figure a quick retreat. My flight was scheduled to leave in less than a half hour. I had delayed going to the boarding area until the last minute hoping to avoid being seen, then that was out. I was a sitting duck if I didn't get away from there quick.

I avoided looking in his direction. I saw people coming through the passageway from an arriving flight. Working my way through the crowd I joined myself to a group meeting an incoming passenger. When they moved toward the escalator - going down to baggage - I followed staying as close to them as I could.

The escalator would make me a target so upon passing a small snack bar I slipped in and found a booth in the rear. The lighting was dim; it was more of a cafe than a fast food place. I felt I might have a few moments of safety here to consider my next move. A shadow fell across the table and the seat opposite became occupied. I again felt those eyes on me. His gun showed over the top of the table. He said, "It's over, get up." That's when I shot him.

I headed for the door as fast as I could move. Just as I reached the passageway I was hit from behind and was on the floor face down, my wrists quickly had metal fastened around them. They pulled me to my feet and it was all over.

That's why I'm here. I'm strapped down on this long narrow table watching a doctor measure the poison that will end this nightmare. People are sitting behind a glass window observing the scene before them. My wife is not there - she was one of the ones I killed and am here for. Getting tired now, this.. is.... how..... it...... ends.............

I Am From

I am from European stock, German and French.

I am from the woods of Pennsylvania, New Jersey's sunny beaches of Atlantic City, majestic mountains and sunshine of California, foggy avenues of London, Deserts of New Mexico wind and rain.

I am from the Great Depression, bread lines, the Hindenburg, World War II, blackouts, rationing, defense plants, P-38's, camouflage, Air Raid Wardens, and VICTORY.

I am from sauerkraut and knockwurst, lemon meringue pies, potato pancakes, Limburger cheese, picnics, the Fourth of July, Christmas get-togethers, and Easter Egg Hunts.

I loved Sinatra, Glen Miller, Bob Hope, bobby socks, swing, boyfriend jackets, peasant skirts, slacks and Elvis.

I know tears, laughter and death.

I love family, my son and daughter, grandchildren, and great-grandchildren.

I believe John 3:16, The Bible, Billy Graham Crusades and have faith in Christ.

This is what I am.

Jeanne Wray